# WHERE DOES LAUGHTER BEGIN?

## Poems that Play with Language

selected by **Wes Magee**
illustrated by **Marc Vyvyan-Jones**

 LONGMAN

# CONTENTS

Bong!

# Where Does Laughter Begin?

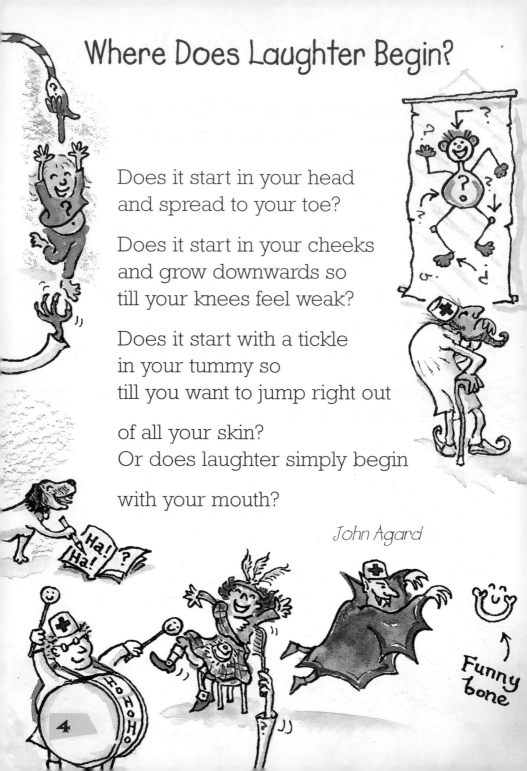

Does it start in your head
and spread to your toe?

Does it start in your cheeks
and grow downwards so
till your knees feel weak?

Does it start with a tickle
in your tummy so
till you want to jump right out

of all your skin?
Or does laughter simply begin

with your mouth?

*John Agard*

Ha!
Ha! ?

HoHoHo

4

Funny
bone

# There Was An Old Woman

There was an old woman of Chester-le-Street
Who chased a policeman all over his beat.

She shattered his helmet and tattered
   his clothes
And knocked his new spectacles clean
   off his nose.

"I'm afraid," said the Judge, "I must make
   it quite clear
You can't get away with that sort of thing here."

"I can and I will," the old woman she said,
"And I don't give a fig for your water
   and bread.

"I don't give a hoot for your cold prison cell,
And your bolts and your bars and your
   handcuffs as well.

"I've never been one to do just as I'm bid.
You can put me in jail for a year!"
   So they did.

*Charles Causley*

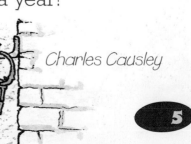

This one bites

5

# Doctors

Dr Aft is rough and ready.
Dr Unk's a bit unsteady.

Dr Omedary's got the hump.
Dr Ift's a snowy bump.

Dr Aught's a shivery chap.
Dr Owsy likes to nap.

Dr Um beats out a roll.
Dr Iver's in control.

Dr Agon's a fiery fighter.
Dr Acula's a late-night biter!

*John Foster*

# I'm Just Going Out For A Moment

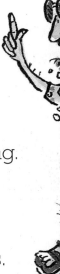

I'm just going out for a moment.
Why?
To make a cup of tea.
Why?
Because I'm thirsty.
Why?
Because it's hot.
Why?
Because the sun's shining.
Why?
Because it's summer.
Why?
Because that's when it is.
Why?
Why don't you stop saying why?
Why?
Tea-time. That's why.
High-time-you-stopped-saying-why-time.
What?

*Michael Rosen*

# A Busy Day

Pop in
pop out
pop over the road
pop out for a walk
pop in for a talk
pop down to the shop
can't stop
got to pop

got to pop?
pop where?
pop what?

well
I've got to
pop round
pop up
pop in to town
pop out and see
pop in for tea
pop down to the shop
can't stop
got to pop

got to pop?
pop where?
pop what?

well
I've got to
pop in
pop out
pop over the road
pop out for a walk
pop in for a talk....

*Michael Rosen*

# Old Gillow

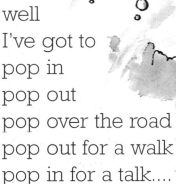

Old Gillow
skin sallow
cheeks hollow
eyes yellow
can't swallow
breath shallow
pains follow
poor fellow!

*Sue Cowling*

# The Mammoth

Gee up, Nellie!...

The mammoth is strong,
The mammoth is brave.
But dear, oh dear,
He could do with a shave.

*Tom Stanier*

# Sabretooth

Sabretooth, oh Sabretooth,
You really are spectacular.
Sabretooth, oh Sabretooth,
You're very like Count Dracula.

*Tom Stanier*

# Singapore Sausage Cat

Behold the cat
the cat full of sausage
his ears do slope backwards
his coat's full of glossage

His whiskers extend
like happy antennae
he would count his
   blessings
but they are too many

He unfoldeth his limbs
he displayeth his fur
he narrows his eyes
and begins to purr

And his purring is
   smooth
as an old tree's
   mossage –
Behold the cat
who is full of
   sausage

*Adrian Mitchell*

# Fish Fingers

Fish Fingers was a clever fish
   much smarter than the rest,
At picking fishes' pockets
   he really was the best.
He pinched a pound from a codling,
   a tenner from a crab
   a wallet from a pollack
   and a fiver from a dab.

He once unzipped a kipper
   with a haddock swimming by
And picked a pilchard's pocket
And made an oyster cry.

He stole a crown from Neptune
He pinched a mermaid's clothes
Pushed messes in her tresses
And winkles up her nose!

The coastguards got all angry
And they caught him straight away
Whilst stealing silver starfish
In a little sandy bay.

They served him with a summons
                   some peas
                   and mushy chips
And that's the end of Fingers, and his nasty little
                   tricks.

*Peter Dixon*

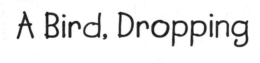

# A Bird, Dropping

There's no stopping
A bird dropping.

*Brian Patten*

# My Dog's First Poem
## (to be read in a dog's voice)

My barking drives them
up the wall.
I chew the carpet
in the hall.
I love to chase
a bouncing ...... banana?

Everywhere I leave
long hairs.
I fight the cushions
on the chairs.
Just watch me race
right up the ...... shower?

Once I chewed
a stick of chalk.
I get bored when
the family talk.
Then someone takes me
for a ....... wheelbarrow?

*Wes Magee*

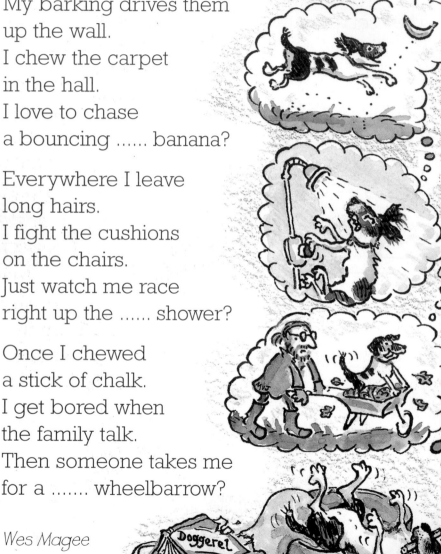

# Hair We Go Again

thin it
trim it
cut it  dye it
curl it  dry
set it
spray

clip it
comb it  mess it
spike it  mousse it
style  wax it
wave  cream it
crimp it
scrunch it
shave

Wet it
wash it
blow it
braid

streak it
shine it
perm it
plait

push it
up in –
side a
hat

*Gina Douthwaite*

15

# Great-Uncle Bertie

Our Great-Uncle Bertie can give you a scare
By perching himself on the back of your chair.
He thinks he's a budgie, and wants to be fed
With almonds and pieces of dry toasted bread.

He nudges his mirror, he climbs up his cage;
His clothes are incredibly bright for his age.
He calls for attention by nibbling his door,
Or scattering his bird-seed all over the floor.

But when he gets bored with your stay, you can tell –
He shows you by sticking his head in his bell.

*John Yeoman*

# Wasps

Wasps like coffee.
Syrup.
Tea.
Coca-Cola.
Butter.
Me.

*Dorothy Aldis*

# Willy The Wizard's Shopping Trip

On Saturday, Willy the Wizard
went into town to do his weekly shopping.

He bought vanishing cream from Roots the
    Alchemist,
a star-spangled cape from Sparks and Mensa,
a new box of tricks from Ploys 'R' Us,
and twenty-four tins of bats' blood soup
from the supermarket – Asda Cadabra!

Then, he met his friend Don Dracula
for a bite at the Burper King,
before picking up a new cauldron
from 'Voodoo It All – The Druid Yourself Store'.

*Paul Cookson*

# What Teacher Did
# On Her Holidays

I cannot bear rude children...

She flew a plane and looped the loop
She dropped her glasses in the soup
She knitted a jumper without arms
She set off Sainsbury's fire alarms
She played for Spurs and scored a goal
She made rock cakes and a sausage roll
She went to the zoo and was chased by a bear
She lost her marbles down the back of a chair
She went for a swim and was swept out to sea
She was rescued by a chimpanzee
She beat Steve Davis and potted the black
Good morning teacher
We're glad you're back.

*Roger Stevens*

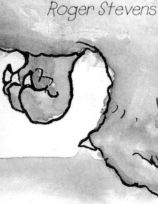

# Literalist

R U A B I C?

O O U R A B!

*John Fandel*

# Where Are They?

"You've got your brother's hair!"
Said Auntie Claire.

"You've got your sister's nose!"
Said Auntie Rose.

I shook my head.

"Not me," I said.
"I haven't touched them –
Honest!"

*Trevor Harvey*

# Don't Call Alligator Long-Mouth Till You Cross River

Call alligator long-mouth
call alligator saw-mouth
call alligator pushy-mouth
call alligator scissors-mouth
call alligator raggedy-mouth
call alligator bumpy-bum
call alligator all dem rude word
but better wait
   till you cross river.

*John Agard*

# Beware!

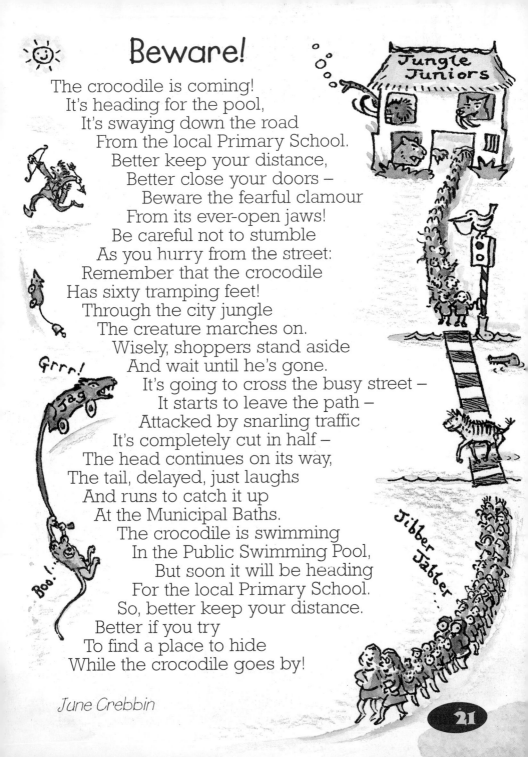

The crocodile is coming!
It's heading for the pool,
It's swaying down the road
From the local Primary School.
Better keep your distance,
Better close your doors –
Beware the fearful clamour
From its ever-open jaws!
Be careful not to stumble
As you hurry from the street:
Remember that the crocodile
Has sixty tramping feet!
Through the city jungle
The creature marches on.
Wisely, shoppers stand aside
And wait until he's gone.
It's going to cross the busy street –
It starts to leave the path –
Attacked by snarling traffic
It's completely cut in half –
The head continues on its way,
The tail, delayed, just laughs
And runs to catch it up
At the Municipal Baths.
The crocodile is swimming
In the Public Swimming Pool,
But soon it will be heading
For the local Primary School.
So, better keep your distance.
Better if you try
To find a place to hide
While the crocodile goes by!

*June Crebbin*

# On The Ning Nang Nong

On the Ning Nang Nong
Where the Cows go Bong!
And the Monkeys all say Boo!
There's a Nong Nang Ning
Where the trees go Ping!
And the tea pots Jibber Jabber Joo.
On the Nong Ning Nang
All the mice go Clang!
And you just can't catch 'em when they do!
So it's Ning Nang Nong!
Cows go Bong!
Nong Nang Ning!
Trees go Ping!
Nong Ning Nang!
The mice go Clang!
What a noisy place to belong,
Is the Ning Nang Ning Nang Nong!

*Spike Milligan*

# Spaghetti

The trouble with
spaghetti is
it gets you in
a fearful tizz,
for when you turn
it round and round
until you think
you've got it wound,
no matter how
you twizzle it, you always get one dangling bit.

One day I'll follow all the bends until I've found a pair of ends.

*Noel Petty*

# Three Riddled Riddles

1.
I have nine legs.
I carry an umbrella.
I live in a box
at the bottom of a ship.
At night
I play the trombone.
What am I?

Answer: I've forgotten.

2.
You see me at dawn
with the clouds in my hair.
I run like a horse
and sing like a nightingale.
I collect stamps
and coconuts.
What am I?

Answer: I'm not sure.

3.
I taste like a grapefruit.
I swim like a chair.
I hang on the trees
and people tap my face,
rake my soil
and tell me jokes.
What am I?

Answer:  I've really no idea.

*Martyn Wiley and Ian McMillan*

# Back Yard, July Night

Firefly, airplane, satellite, star –
How I wonder which you are.

*William Cole*

# The Day The Dragons Won The Lottery

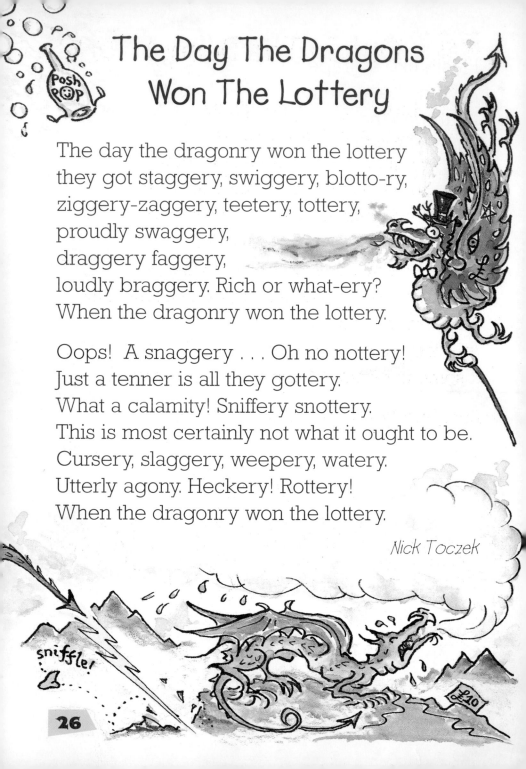

The day the dragonry won the lottery
they got staggery, swiggery, blotto-ry,
ziggery-zaggery, teetery, tottery,
proudly swaggery,
draggery faggery,
loudly braggery. Rich or what-ery?
When the dragonry won the lottery.

Oops!  A snaggery . . . Oh no nottery!
Just a tenner is all they gottery.
What a calamity! Sniffery snottery.
This is most certainly not what it ought to be.
Cursery, slaggery, weepery, watery.
Utterly agony. Heckery! Rottery!
When the dragonry won the lottery.

*Nick Toczek*

#  Out In The Desert

Out in the desert lies the sphinx
It never eats and it never drinx
Its body quite solid without any chinx
And when the sky's all purples and pinx
(As if it was painted with coloured inx)
And the sun it ever so swiftly sinx
Behind the hills in a couple of twinx
You may hear (if you're lucky) a bell that clinx
And also tolls and also tinx
And they say at the very same sound the sphinx
It sometimes smiles and it sometimes winx:

But nobody knows just what it thinx.

*Charles Causley*

# Names Of Scottish Islands To Be Shouted In A Bus Queue When You're Feeling Bored

Yell!
Muck!
Eigg!
Rhum!
Unst!
Hoy!
Foula!
Coll!
Canna!
Barra!
Gigha!
Jura!
Pabay!
Raasay!
Skye!

*Ian McMillan*

# That Sinking Feeling

He rocked the boat,
did Ezra Shank;
These bubbles mark

O
O
O
O
O
O
O
O
O
O
O
O
O
O
O
O
O
O

Where Ezra sank.

*Anonymous*

# Mud

It squelches and belches
A spattering flop
A morass of dense goop
That gurges in glops

Now seeping now weeping
A popple a spurt
A lagoon of brown pudding
Some very wet dirt

It burbles so blustery
And spills out its custardy
Bubbles that pop
From bottom to top

To squeeze between toes
And squish as it goes
All oozy and flabby
Dank deep and slabby

Oh
No
So
Slow

What a lazy muddle
What a hiccup of a puddle

*Zaro Weil*

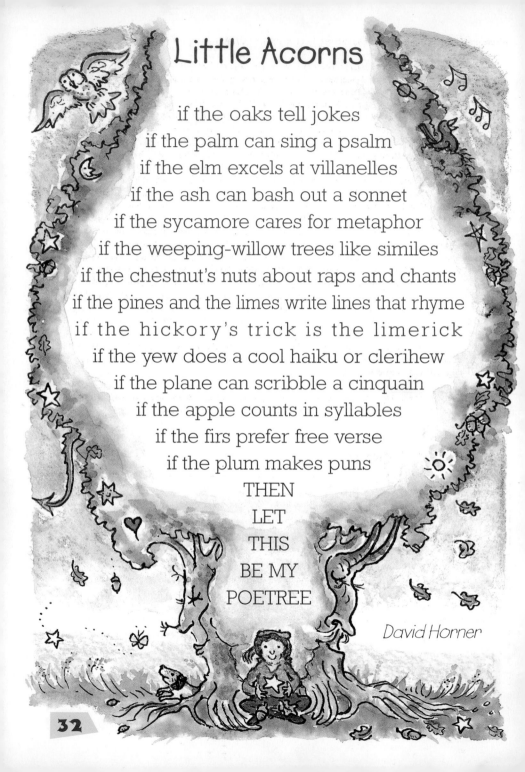

# Little Acorns

if the oaks tell jokes
if the palm can sing a psalm
if the elm excels at villanelles
if the ash can bash out a sonnet
if the sycamore cares for metaphor
if the weeping-willow trees like similes
if the chestnut's nuts about raps and chants
if the pines and the limes write lines that rhyme
if the hickory's trick is the limerick
if the yew does a cool haiku or clerihew
if the plane can scribble a cinquain
if the apple counts in syllables
if the firs prefer free verse
if the plum makes puns
THEN
LET
THIS
BE MY
POETREE

*David Horner*